Make way for the monsters from
MONSTER MANOR

MONSTER MANOR
Sally Gets Silly

by PAUL MARTIN and MANU BOISTEAU
Adapted by LISA PAPADEMETRIOU
Illustrated by MANU BOISTEAU

Hyperion Books for Children
New York

visit us at www.abdopublishing.com

Reinforced library bound edition published in 2012 by Spotlight,
a division of ABDO Publishing Group, 8000 West 78th Street, Edina,
Minnesota 55439. Spotlight produces high-quality reinforced library
bound editions for schools and libraries. This edition reprinted
by arrangement with Disney Book Group, LLC.

Printed in the United States of America, Melrose Park, Illinois.
052011
092011

 This book contains at least 10% recycled materials.

First published under the title *Maudit Manoir, Pas de repos
pour Céleste!* in France by Bayard Jeunesse. © Bayard Editions
Jeunesse, 2002 Text copyright © 2002 by Paul Martin
Illustrations copyright © 2002 by Manu Boisteau Monster Manor and
the Volo colophon are trademarks of Disney Enterprises, Inc.
Volo® is a registered trademark of Disney Enterprises, Inc.
Volo/Hyperion Books for Children are imprints of
Disney Children's Book Group, L.L.C.

Library of Congress Cataloging-in-Publication Data

This title was previously cataloged with the following information:

Martin, Paul, 1968-
Sally gets silly / by Paul Martin and Manu Boisteau ;
adapted by Lisa Papademetriou ; illustrated by Manu Boisteau.
p. cm. -- (Monster Manor ; #7)
[1. Monsters --Fiction.]
I. Boisteau, Manu. II. Papademetriou, Lisa. III. Title. IV. Series.
PZ7.M3641833 Sal 2003
[FIC]--dc22
                    2005295538
ISBN 978-1-59961-888-3 (reinforced library bound edition)

All Spotlight books are reinforced library bindings
and manufactured in the United States of America.

Contents

If you're ever in Transylvaniaville, be sure to stop by Mon Staire Manor. Everyone calls it *Monster* Manor... that's because a bunch of monsters live there.

The Haunted Hills

Nerdburg

Transylvaniaville

Malibu Nightclub

MALIBU

A Scary-looking Tree

The Slippen Falls

There are lots of fun things to do at the Manor. You can stroll through the cemetery, watch the swamp glow under the moonlight, or make a few new friends!

The FEMUR Family

EYE-GORE & STEVE

This sweet little family may look scary, but the truth is that they have no guts at all.

They want to be skate punks, but they're really just zombies with bad attitudes.

BEATRICE Mon Staire
She's haunted by a horrible secret... and a hairdo that's even worse.

Wolf Man STU
When the moon is full, he becomes human. Well, *somewhat* human...

COUNT SNOBULA
He isn't rich, but he *is* totally stuck up. Thank goodness he sleeps all day.

Step through the gate— let's see who's home!

The SWAMP HORROR

SALLY the Specter

Professor VON SKALPEL

It ain't easy being a big green ball of toxic slime!

Beatrice's mother is smart, sassy—and a ghost!

The most brilliant mad scientist in town. He's a real cutup.

FRANKIE

Created by Von Skalpel,
Frankie is one of a kind.
Thank goodness.

If you dare come inside, bring earplugs.
Sally likes to toot her own horn!

CHAPTER ONE
The Day the TV Died

Soupy fog settled over the sleepy village of Transylvaniaville. Not a sound came from the dark Manor at the top of the hill. Usually, the villagers lived in fear of Mon Staire Manor. They called it Monster Manor and said that the screaming and stomping that came from the house at night were the work of terrible vampires, hideous creatures, beasts, skeletons, witches, ghosts, and a very short, mad scientist with a weird accent.

Naturally, that was all perfectly true. But right now, everything was quiet. Too quiet.

Suddenly, a horrible scream cut through the fog.

"Dead!" a voice shouted. "The werewolf killed it!"

"Oh, be quiet, Bonehead!" Wolf Man Stu said to the little skeleton beside him. He wasn't being rude—Bonehead was the skeleton's name. The werewolf bared his fangs at the blank television screen. "Listen up, you!" Wolf Man Stu shouted at the TV. "You'd better turn on in time for us to watch *Eat Something Gross!* or you'll find yourself dealing with a ferocious wolf man!"

The television did not reply.

"Stu," said Count Snobula, who was an old vampire in a tattered cape, "I really don't think that's going to—"

Wolf Man Stu hurled the remote at the TV screen. There was a crash, and then a hiss. The TV sparked a little and belched black smoke.

"—Work," Count Snobula finished.

Wolf Man Stu folded his arms across his chest. "That'll show you," he said to the TV.

"You've killed our beautiful television!" wailed Steve, one of the zombies.

"Let this be on your head," added his brother, Eye-Gore, who glared at Stu so

Wolf Man Stu really blew it this time!

fiercely that one of his eyeballs bounced at the end of its stalk.

"What are we going to do now?" asked the goopy, slimy creature known as the Swamp Horror. He had turned an extra-vibrant shade of green. "We love that TV!"

"Hello, everyvun!" Professor Von Skalpel, the mad scientist, sang as he walked into the room. His handmade creation and assistant, Frankie, loped along behind him. "I hope you do not mind, but I had to borrow zee batteries from zee remote control for one of my experiments! But I brought us some new vuns—here zey are!"

Everyone stared at the TV, which continued to pour out thick smoke.

"Um, I think I jutht figured out why the televithion wouldn't turn on," Bonehead lisped. Bonehead had a pretty horrible lisp, but it didn't stop him from being quite the little chatterbox.

"Vhat have you done to zee TV?" Von Skalpel shouted. He was the one who had donated the ancient set to the house in the first place. "Vhat are vee going to do now?"

"We could talk to each other," Frankie suggested.

Snobula glared at him. "How dare you suggest something so horrible?" he demanded.

"Hey, everyone!" chirped a cheerful voice. "Turn those frowns upside down—I've got something much better than TV! Check this out!"

"Mother!" shouted Beatrice Mon Staire, the owner of the Manor. "You're invisible again!"

"Ooops!" Sally suddenly appeared in the middle of the room. "Sorry, I forgot." Sally

was a ghost,
and she could turn
invisible whenever she
wanted. Usually she turned invisible only
when she felt like cheating at cards or spying
on people. Right now, she was holding an old
movie projector. "Who wants to see old movies
of Beatrice when she was little?" Sally asked
eagerly.

"Mother!" Beatrice cried, embarrassed by

the thought of all the residents watching her. "Nobody wants to see that!"

"Cool! Let's check out Beatrice's old-school hairdos!" Steve shouted.

"Oh, yeah—and didn't Beatrith wear head-gear?" Bonehead asked. "Thith'll be great!"

"See, sweetie?" Sally said to her daughter as she set up the projector on a table. "Everyone wants to watch!" Sally flipped on the projector, and the pictures leaped to life.

There was Beatrice at age six, an adorable little girl with black ribbons and purple spiders in her hair. She was throwing a horrible tantrum while a tall man behind her smiled warmly.

"Who is the gentleman?" Snobula asked. "Beatrice's father?"

"No way!" Sally said with a giggle. "Beatrice's dad always had to lie down with a headache whenever Beatrice had a fit. No, the only one who could stand to be near her was our robot, Harry. It was odd—Harry was a real jerk, but with Beatrice, he was a big sweetie. He was just crazy about her."

A new image popped up. Beatrice was slightly older, and was, in fact, wearing head-gear like the kind Bonehead had mentioned. In the movie, she was sitting with a small green gremlin, eating a slice of cockroach pie.

"Hey—that's Fred!" shouted Wolf Man Stu. "He nearly got rid of us all in book three!"

"Oooh, maybe take smaller bites next time," Eye-Gore said as the on-screen Beatrice got a cockroach stuck in her braces.

"Okay, Mother," Beatrice said as she rose from her chair. "I think everyone's seen quite enough."

"No, no—wait!" Sally cried. "The funniest

part of all is coming right up!"

The scene flickered, and now Fred was pointing to a book, and Beatrice was reading aloud.

"She's trying to turn him into a frog!" Sally explained.

On-screen, Beatrice finished reading, then looked confused. Fred hadn't changed. Beatrice opened her mouth, and a three-foot-long tongue flopped out.

The monsters cracked up.

"Hee-hee!" The professor giggled loudly. "Vhat is zee matter, Beatrice?" he said. "Do

you have a frog in your sroat?"

"Next up, Beatrice tries her first beauty potion!" Sally cried.

"Don't you dare!" Beatrice shouted, lunging across the room. She didn't want anyone to see her with a pig snout and a beard! Quick as lightning, Beatrice grabbed the reel from the projector and ran out of the room.

"Hmmm . . ." Wolf Man Stu said as he watched Beatrice run up the stairs. "She seems kind of mad. . . ."

Sally shrugged and shook her head. "That girl has the worst temper," she said. "I'll go talk to her." She headed up the stairs.

Dong-dong-dong-dong! Do-o-o-o-o-ong!

The professor looked at the door. "I vill get it," he said. "It sounds important."

He had no idea how right he was.

CHAPTER TWO
Beatrice Gets Down

Beatrice slammed her bedroom door and stalked over to the bookshelf that held her most powerful spells. As usual, she ignored all of those books and reached for the CDs on the bottom shelf. Beatrice was a lousy witch. She knew that trying to punish her mother with magic would probably just backfire.

No—what she needed was to listen to her favorite singer of all time. The singer's name was Mister-E-Us, and he was very mysterious.

His CDs never showed a single photograph of him.

"I bet he's really handsome," Beatrice thought. "But he doesn't want people to judge him only by his gorgeous looks."

Beatrice turned on the CD player and flopped down on her spiderweb bedspread as the music poured from the speakers.

Baby, you're like a mad, mad scientist,
Shouting in the lab of love!
Making up creatures, like in the scary features,
And cooking up concoctions on the stove!

Beatrice took a deep breath and sighed. Mister-E-Us's songs always spoke to her.

"Beeeeee-a-trice!" called a syrupy voice. "May I come in?" Sally asked as she poked her head through the closed door.

"Mother!" Beatrice shouted. "Don't you ever knock?"

"Sorry," Sally said as she stepped through the door, "but I guess it's too late now."

Beatrice rolled her eyes.

"Come on, sweetie," Sally urged. "Come downstairs and play Go Fish with us."

"No way," Beatrice said. "I never want to see any of those monsters again. It's bad enough that you became a ghost. You broke Daddy's heart—no wonder he left! And then Harry and Fred

disappeared. But now I have to live with a bunch of low-class creatures. And to top it off—you embarrassed me in front of them!"

"Well, they're not *all* low-class," Sally said.

Beatrice sighed. "I just wish that I could be near someone artistic—someone creative—someone like . . ."

Just then, a new song started.

They say, "Use it or lose it,"
So I'd better move it,
And sneak this old chicken into the
soup tonight!
So what if it's hairy,
Blue, green, and scary?

Once it's in the soup, this chicken's
  gonna delight!

"Someone like this singer!" Beatrice cried. "Mister-E-Us is classy, and I bet he can really dance. That's who I should be hanging out with—not zombies and creatures stitched together from old body parts."

Sally grinned. She happened to know for a fact that Mister-E-Us was none other than Frankie, Professor Von Skalpel's clumsy assistant. *It's amazing what you can find out when you're invisible,* Sally thought. She decided to keep that a secret for now.

"Just leave me alone," Beatrice wailed.

The CD seemed to agree:

Leave me alone!
Hanging by the phone!

Let me wail and moan!
'Cause the pizza man don't deliver past
   midnight.

Sally dropped through the floor and into the living room. Everybody was still there.

"Skalpie," Sally called, "why don't you fix the TV? You're the genius of the house."

"Professor Von Skalpel isn't here," Horror said. "He went to answer the door a while ago, and hasn't come back."

"Hmmm . . ." Sally rubbed her chin. "Interesting."

Sally always liked to have something to investigate. She headed off to start snooping.

CHAPTER THREE
Sally Starts Spying

Sally floated carefully through the fog that hung outside the Manor. It was so misty that it would have been difficult to see her—even if she hadn't been invisible, which she was. Up ahead, by the gate to the Manor, she spotted the professor. He must have stepped outside, Sally thought.

"Fine!" Professor Von Skalpel said to a large and mysterious man, "Zee second vun from above? All right—I vill take care of it!

Tell your boss he can have it in zee morning."

The large man retreated into the mist and the professor turned back toward the Manor. He was smiling.

Sally frowned. Professor Von Skalpel had a large, goofy grin on his face.

Old Skalpie has something up his sleeve, Sally said to herself. I wonder what it is. And what it has to do with Beatrice's room.

The professor whistled cheerfully as he headed toward the house.

Whatever it is, it must be something truly awful, Sally thought. She hurried after the professor, stepping through the front door as he fumbled with the doorknob. Sally stopped in the entranceway and made herself visible again.

"Oh, hello, Professor!" Sally chirped when Von Skalpel walked into the Manor, as though she were surprised to see him. "I just came down from talking to Beatrice."

"Ah, yes," the professor said, smiling. "And how is zee poor lady?"

"Oh, she's just sulking," Sally said with a shrug. "You know how she can get. It's only a matter of time before she starts acting as if nothing happened. Mark my words, by this time next year, she'll come out of that room and feel like throwing a party."

The professor's eyes bulged behind his dark glasses. "Zis time next year?" he cried. "She vill not stay locked in her room all zat time, vill she?"

"Oh, sure!" Sally said. "Remember when she asked Frankie to paint the front of the Manor, but didn't tell him what color to use?"

"Ah, yes," Professor Von Skalpel said, stroking his beard. "I remember. He used zat awful Pepto-Bismol-pink color."

"And Beatrice sulked for eight months," Sally finished. "Then one day, she came down from her room, fixed herself a peanut-butter-and-anchovy sandwich, and never said a word about the paint again!"

"Hmmm . . . has she alvays been zis vay?" the professor asked.

"It got worse after Allsaint left," Sally admitted.

The professor's ears perked up. He had never been able to figure out why Sally's husband, Allsaint Mon Staire, had left the Manor. Everyone had a theory. Snobula said that it was because Beatrice was such a horrible witch that Allsaint was embarrassed. The zombies claimed that he had left after Transylvania-ville's snakeball team was sold to Cleveland. And Wolf Man Stu claimed that Allsaint had never really existed at all. The professor wasn't sure he believed any of those stories.

"Vhat exactly *did* happen to your husband?" the professor asked.

"Oh," Sally said, waving her hand dismissively, "that's a boring story. By the way, who was at the door earlier?"

The professor turned bright red. "Er—vhat?" he asked. He leaned against the banister in an attempt to act casual, but missed it by three inches and nearly fell over.

"Didn't you answer the door earlier?" Sally asked innocently. "I was sure that Frankie said you did."

"Oh—right. Zat vas a . . . uh . . . mattress salesman. He vas selling . . . uh . . . mattresses. Yes, zat is right."

"In the middle of the night?"

"Vell . . . zat is zee best time for sleeping, is it not?" the professor asked brightly.

Sally's mouth twisted up into a half smile. The professor was lying. . . . but why?

"Vell, it's getting late," Professor Von Skalpel said as he glanced at his watch. "Vow—eight fifty-five already! I am off to bed. I vill see you later, Sa—"

But Sally disappeared before the professor finished. She had to get to the Ghost Office before it closed.

CHAPTER FOUR
The Ghost Office

The Ghost Office was a gloomy place. It wasn't quite in the living world, but it wasn't quite in the world of the dead, either. It was sort of like a train station on the edge of town—just the first stop on the path to wherever it was you were going. The only problem was . . . you never seemed to get anywhere. Also, it had dingy, vinyl floors, a thick layer of dust that lay over everything, and horrible lights that made everyone look pale.

Sally sighed and peered at the plaque outside the door, which read:

OFFICIAL GHOST OFFICE

HOURS: LAST FRIDAY OF EVERY ODD

MONTH, FROM 9:00 P.M. TO 9:30 P.M.

Pushing open the door, Sally stepped into the crowded room. Ghosts of every age, shape, and size stood in a line that wrapped around the room twice. Sally shook her head and walked to the end of the line. She hated the sickly, green color of the room. It always made

her hair seem extra purple.

"Next!" called the short, bald, almost transparent ghost behind the glass. His name, according to his name tag, was Uriah Phantom. He had been working at the Ghost Office as long as Sally could remember. He wasn't very good at his job, but he was an official employee of the State of Death, so he couldn't get fired. "Next!" he repeated testily.

Sally glanced at the walls as the line shuffled forward. There were posters everywhere advertising the Next World. Most of them 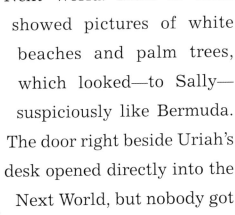 showed pictures of white beaches and palm trees, which looked—to Sally— suspiciously like Bermuda. The door right beside Uriah's desk opened directly into the Next World, but nobody got into it without Uriah's official stamp. That was why everyone was waiting in line—they had all been cursed in one way or another, and they couldn't get into the Next World without completing a task. Nobody got a stamp until his or her task was complete.

"Excuse me," said the ghost in front of Sally. He was large and looked strong—a handsome phantom, Sally thought, smiling. "Would you help me figure out this form?"

"Sure." Sally plucked the pink paper from the ghost's hand. It stated that the ghost wanted to go to the Next World. Sally glanced at the form. "Is your name really Frank Furter?"

"Of course it's not!" the ghost snapped. "Someone typed that name into the computer, and it's been wrong in the system ever since! Frank Furter. Thank goodness that isn't my

The coffee here is terrible. . . .

PFF

name—it's ridiculous."

"Okay," Sally said, pulling out a pen. "So what is your name?"

"Frank Farter," he replied, matter-of-factly.

Sally snorted to keep herself from laughing. "Um . . . okay, I see that your profession is—swimmer?"

"Five-time Olympic champion," Frank bragged.

Sally frowned. "I've never heard of you."

"Yes, well—I won the Best Attitude award three times, and Most Improved twice," Frank explained.

"Okay," Sally said, "it says that to get your passage, you had to save five . . ." The paper was smudged, Sally couldn't quite make out the word. "Five *somethings* from drowning."

"Five logs," Frank said.

"Logs? How were you going to do that?"

"It wasn't easy, let me tell you. I started haunting this campground near a lake. Every time people gathered wood for a fire, I would wait for one to fall off the pile. If it rolled toward the lake, I leaped in and caught it. But that didn't happen very often. It took me seventeen years to save just five logs! And now they're saying that I've done something wrong—that I can't go to the Next World."

Sally looked back down at the page. "Well, I think I see the problem. This might actually say 'dogs,' not 'logs,'" she said slowly.

Frank's eyes grew wide with shock. "What?" he demanded. "Dogs?"

"Well . . ." Sally said hesitantly, "yeah."

"You're kidding!" Frank cried. "Dogs were

always jumping in that lake. But I never paid attention to them unless they were chasing a large, loglike stick. Now I have to start all over!"

Just then, a new ghost glided into the room and came to stand behind Sally.

Frank leaned toward Sally and whispered, "Act natural."

"Okay," Sally said. She wasn't sure how else she could act.

"The guy behind you is Harry Helmet, the race-car driver," Frank explained. "In life, he always came in first, but now he has to wait at the end of the line forever. They say he'll never get to the window before it closes."

"How awful!" Sally cried.

"Next!" Uriah cried frantically.

"Your turn," Sally told Frank. Frank moved up to the window.

Frank argued his case, but Uriah wasn't

interested in how many logs Frank had saved. "The form says 'dogs,'" Uriah insisted. "I can't give you credit for your logs. I'm sorry."

Frank sighed and shuffled away.

"Next!" Uriah shouted.

Sally stepped up to the window and handed over a lavender-colored piece of paper. Uriah looked at it.

"*Sally Mon Staire,*" Uriah read. "*You must haunt Mon Staire Manor until you've made peace with your family.* I see you're having trouble with your daughter, Beatrice."

"She's difficult," Sally said with a sigh.

"Hmmm," Uriah grunted.

Please don't poke your head through the glass.

"She still listening to those CDs?"

"All the time," Sally said.

Uriah plastered a large REJECTED stamp on her form. "Come back in two months, as usual."

"See you!" Sally said with a smile. The truth was, she didn't care about getting into the Next World very much. She liked the Manor. All of her friends were there. It was a far more fun place than this dreary office, that was for sure.

"Next!" Uriah cried.

The ghost behind Sally let out a cry of joy and stepped up to the window.

"Why, if it isn't Harry Helmet," Uriah said. "The champion racer!"

"That's right!" Harry cried. "And my curse has finally ended—I'm at the front of the line again!"

"Well, congratulations!" Uriah told him.

"Would you mind autographing a photo for me? My daughter is a big fan of yours."

"Sure." Harry pulled out his library card, which had his photograph on the front, and scrawled his name across the picture. He handed it to Uriah.

"Thanks," Uriah said. "Now you can get your passage into the Next World. I just need to see the appropriate documents."

Harry pulled out several forms. "Here's my Passage Request."

Uriah stamped it.

"Here's my death certificate," Harry went on, "and here's my—" He slapped at his pockets. "Wait—I just gave you my only photo I.D."

"Oh, well, that's too bad," Uriah said. "I need to attach your photo to the forms. You'll have to come back in two months."

"Couldn't you just give me back my library

card?" Harry asked hopefully.

"What?" Uriah demanded. "That's for my daughter! Come back in two months." With that, Uriah slammed down the metal gate between himself and the window.

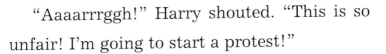

"Aaaarrrggh!" Harry shouted. "This is so unfair! I'm going to start a protest!"

Sally ducked out the door as several ghosts stepped forward, eager to hear Harry's protest. She knew that it was a lost cause. But Harry had just given her an excellent idea for how to make up with Beatrice.

CHAPTER FIVE
Sally Stirs Things Up

A few moments later, Sally stuck her head through Frankie's wall. "Frankie!" she whispered.

"Yikes!" Frankie shouted, tossing his little pink notebook into the air. He had been plucking at his guitar and scribbling—writing songs, no doubt. "Uh—hello, Mrs. Mon Staire. I was just cleaning a friend's musical instrument."

Sally walked into the room. "Don't be

silly," Sally said. "I've known about your little secret for ages."

Frankie stared at her, wide-eyed. "You mean about the clock?" he asked. "I didn't mean to bash it—that clock started it!"

"No, not that secret," Sally said, shaking her head. "I know that you're Mister-E-Us."

"Well, thanks," Frankie said, "nobody's ever told me that I was mysterious before."

"No, Frankie. I know that you're Mister-E-Us, the singer!" Sally corrected. "I know that you have a recording studio in the basement. And I know that you get sacks of fan mail from all over the world."

"Who told you?" Frankie demanded, suspiciously.

Sally rolled her eyes. "Frankie, I can make myself invisible and walk through walls. I know everything that goes on around here."

"Oh, no!" Frankie cried. "Please don't tell. If people find out what I look like, they won't write me any more nice letters!"

"That's okay, your secret's safe with me, sweetie," Sally said. "I just want a little favor. I know someone who loves your music, and I was hoping that you would autograph a CD for her."

Frankie let out such a sigh of relief that the curtains blew down from the windows and a

bedside lamp fell to the floor with a crash. Peering under his bed, he pulled out a box of CDs and picked out one titled *Junk Food of Love*.

"This one is really rare," Frankie said, holding up the disk. "It was recorded for the tenth anniversary of Super Crunchies. There's an ad between every verse. It's a real collector's item."

"It's perfect!" Sally cried. "Here." She handed Frankie a pen.

With a hundred slobbery kisses, Frankie wrote, *from Mister-E-Us to . . .* He looked up at Sally.

"To Beatrice," Sally said.

"Hey! I know a Beatrice, too! How weird," Frankie replied as he scribbled the name on the disk and handed it to Sally.

"Thanks," Sally said holding up the CD.

"I'm sure she'll love it."

Frankie reached down for his pink notebook just as Sally turned to leave. "Uh . . . Mrs. Mon Staire?" Frankie said slowly. "Do you think you could help me with something?"

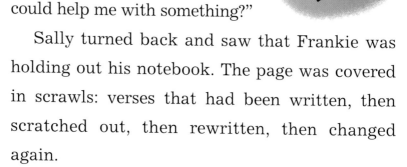

Sally turned back and saw that Frankie was holding out his notebook. The page was covered in scrawls: verses that had been written, then scratched out, then rewritten, then changed again.

"I have to finish this song," Frankie explained, "but I can't make the last verse work."

"Let me see." Sally grabbed the notebook from Frankie and began to read:

Ooooh, I think I need a nurse,
I'm living with a curse,
You don't even know my name!
I'd even stand in goo,
If I could be with you,
And we could play a fun card game!

Ooooh, you're so wonderful,
And I'm so blunderful,
Everything about you simply rocks!
Ooooh, you're so fabulous,
And I'm so scab-u-lous,
That we should . . .

"That we should what?" Sally asked.

"That's the problem!" Frankie cried. "I don't know how to end it."

"Well," Sally said, "you could say, 'That we should have a pizza party.' I just love pizza parties. They're always fun!"

"Hmmm," Frankie thought for a moment, "but it really should rhyme with 'rocks.'"

"So, how about, 'That we should go and find a box?'"

"But that doesn't make any sense!" Frankie cried.

"I thought you wanted it to rhyme!" Sally huffed. "I can't do *everything* for you. Anyway, thanks for the CD."

"You're welcome."

Sally slid the disk under the door before stepping through it, leaving Frankie with his musical mystery.

CHAPTER SIX
Von Skalpel Gets Gassy

The sky turned pink behind Monster Manor as the sun rose, shining down on the still, quiet house. That is, still, and *mostly* quiet. Except for the sound of Wolf Man Stu, howling in his sleep. And Swamp Horror's trumpet practice. And Count Snobula's tap dancing. And the wailing of the zombie brothers' electric guitars.

Other than that, the Manor was completely silent.

But even in this peace and quiet, Sally couldn't get to sleep. She was staring down at her daughter, who hadn't yet woken up. Sally couldn't wait to give the autographed CD to Beatrice. But it looked as though Sally might have to wait a while longer. . . . her daughter's head was buried deep beneath a pile of pillows, and she was snoring like a chain saw.

Sally looked around the room and heaved a heavy sigh. When Sally became a ghost and Allsaint moved away, Beatrice had moved into their room. But the room was still almost exactly the way it had been when Sally and Allsaint had shared it. It was full of mementos.

The bat skeleton that hung over the mirror had been a birthday present from Sally's mother. In the corner was the fifteenth-anniversary present she had given Allsaint—a collection of poisoned arrows from around the

world. It was all right there. Beatrice had left everything in place except the pictures of her parents. She had taken those all down the day that her father had moved away.

Suddenly, a thick, green mist began to stream into the room from the crack beneath the door. In seconds, the mist became a heavy cloud that filled the room.

It doesn't look like smoke, Sally thought. Could it be dangerous? Of course, Sally was a ghost, so she had nothing to worry about. But her daughter . . .

"Beatrice!" Sally shouted. "Wake up!"

Beatrice snored louder.

"Beatrice!" Sally cried, pulling the pile of pillows from her daughter's head. But it was no use. Beatrice was sound asleep.

Just then, a loud noise boomed through the room, shaking the floor. The door flew off its hinges, and two figures—one large and one small and bald—stumbled into the room.

"Frankie, I zought I told you to be careful!"

The voice was muffled, but Sally thought

Oh! Sally, uh . . . vee vere looking for . . . uh, zee bassroom. . . .

she recognized it—there was only one man in the world with such a weird accent: Professor Von Skalpel.

"I *was* careful, Professor!" Frankie said. "They don't make doors like they used to."

That was when Sally noticed that both Frankie and the professor were wearing large face masks. Professor Von Skalpel's jaw dropped when he saw Sally.

"Oh, hi!" the professor said brightly. "It's just us."

Sally folded her arms across her chest and frowned at the professor. "Just what the jibber-jabber is going on here?" she demanded.

"Uh . . ." the professor said slowly, "vell . . . I zought zat—since Beatrice vas so upset— she might like to try my latest invention: zee Grassnorer. Zee smell is very calming."

Sally glanced at her daughter, whose snoring

was louder than ever. "I'll say," Sally agreed.

"It vill vear off in about ten hours or zo," the professor added.

Sally frowned at the door. "But why did you rip the door off the hinges?"

"Oh, vell, you know," Professor Von Skalpel said, waving his hand in the air, "Frankie does not know his own strength."

Frankie looked hurt. "But you told me to break the lock to get in!" he protested.

Von Skalpel drew his finger across his throat in a "cut it out" motion, but Frankie went on, "Do you want to look for—"

In a flash, the professor reached out and yanked off Frankie's mask. The green air seeped inside. Frankie gave a small hiccup, then fell to the floor.

"Oh, sorry!" the professor said. "I sought I saw a bug in zee mask."

Sally narrowed her eyes. One thing was for sure—the professor was acting mighty suspicious, and she wanted to get to

the bottom of it. "What are you really doing here?" she shouted. "What are you looking for? Why did you put Beatrice to sleep? Who was that man you were talking to last night? What did he want? What is the capital of New Jersey? Answer me!"

Von Skalpel stared at her, stunned by the stream of questions. He was caught, and he knew it.

All he could hope for now was some kind of distraction. A tornado, an earthquake, a hurricane—anything!

CHAPTER SEVEN
Anything But That!

Just then, the doorbell rang.

"Oh, no!" Von Skalpel cried. "It is him! And I have not found it!" But the mist was getting thicker, and the professor was still wearing his face mask, so this sounded more like, "Orgho—blith im! Yams around fit!"

"What?" Sally shouted. "I can't understand a word you're saying."

Professor Von Skalpel rolled his eyes and yanked off his face mask. "I *said*—" Then *he* gave a small hiccup and fell to the floor.

"Well, that was dumb," Sally said to herself. The professor had been knocked out by his own gas.

Whoever it was that had rung the bell now began to pound on the door.

Outside, Wolf Man Stu growled and stormed out of his doghouse. "Who's pounding on the door at seven in the morning?" he shouted. "Don't you people know that a ferocious werewolf needs his beauty sleep?"

Wolf Man Stu stomped toward the visitor. He bared his fangs and leaped at the man, chomping down on his leg.

Crunch!

"Ow!" Wolf Man Stu shouted. "This man has a metal leg!"

The stranger kept banging on the door.

The werewolf leaped at the visitor again,

but it didn't seem to make any impact on him. The man was huge and he seemed to be made entirely of steel. He flicked Stu away with one twitch of his meaty finger, opened the door, and stepped into the Manor.

Stu landed in the radioactive swamp. "Okay, okay," Stu called weakly. "I'll go easy on you, because you look familiar." This was actually true. The stranger did look familiar,

but Stu couldn't remember where he had seen him before.

Sally had seen the whole thing from Beatrice's window. "Oh, my gosh!" Sally cried. She turned to her daughter and shook her shoulder. "Beatrice, wake up! You're the only one who can stop him!"

A moment later, there was a terrible *splat*, like the sound of someone diving into a pool full of Jell-O.

"Oh, no—he's run into Horror!" Sally shouted.

"Stop him, Horror!" Sally heard Count Snobula shout. "Not like that. Hmmm . . . how are we ever going to get rid of that mess?"

"Let's get out of here!" Eye-Gore shouted.

Fibula Femur shrieked, "I'm behind you!"

A moment later, heavy footsteps sounded on the stairs.

"He's headed this way!" Sally cried. She crossed the room and gave Frankie a kick. After all, he was the largest monster in the Manor. But Frankie just let out a short snort and rolled over.

Desperate, Sally hurried over to her daughter's bookshelf and put Frankie's latest CD into the stereo. Sally turned the sound all the way up.

Yeah, I'm like a sturgeon,
Hooked on a very short line!

Will you fry me up and gobble me down,
Or sell me for $5.99 a pound?

Super Crunchies taste great with fish!

Like a flounder,
Floundering flounderiferously!
Will you save me from the deep, dark sea,
Or stuff me with crab in a fricassee?

Super Crunchies—with dinner or
     as a snack!

At the sound of a brand-new Mister-E-Us song, Beatrice sat up, wide awake.

"What's that wonderful music?" Beatrice asked.

At that moment, a hulking figure appeared in the doorway, and Sally let out a scream.

CHAPTER EIGHT
Things Get Crazy

Wolf Man Stu sank further into the green ooze of the radioactive swamp. He struggled against the chemical waste of the marsh, but it was no use. He had been hit hard, and could barely breathe.

Would this be the end of Wolf Man Stu?

Wait a minute—let me check.

Um . . . hmmm . . . okay—I think it might— oh, no, wait. He has a line on the last page.

Okay. So, just then, Stu felt someone grab

him by the tail. A powerful grip lifted him, dripping and gross, into the air.

"I did it!" a voice cried. "I got one!"

A moment later, Stu was sitting on the bank, spitting out mud and small, froglike creatures. "Blech!" Stu said. "Dis-*gusting*!"

"Wait a minute," said the handsome guy from the Ghost Office, who had suddenly appeared on the scene. "You can talk? Does that mean you're not a dog?"

"I'm a werewolf," Stu told him.

Frank Farter sighed. "I'll never get this right!" he griped, and disappeared.

Stu took a deep breath and looked toward the Manor, where he caught sight of the metal man. It looked as though he were running away. But that monster was bigger and stronger than anyone in the Manor, Stu thought. Who could have driven him out?

Frankie? Swamp Horror? Some new, hideous creature invented by that lunatic Professor Von Skalpel?

At that moment, Beatrice stomped out of the Manor, shouting, "And stay out!"

Horror bounded out after her and wrapped her in a big hug. "Way to go, Bea!"

"You told him!" Count Snobula said, trotting up after Horror.

"Let's go tell everyone what happened!" Horror said brightly.

"Oooh, this is so exciting!" Snobula said as he and Horror headed for the cemetery. "No one will be able to believe it."

Beatrice grinned proudly, then turned to her mother, who had appeared at Beatrice's elbow. "Thanks, Mom."

Sally's eyebrows flew up. "For what?"

"For waking me up in time to send Harry the Robot away," Beatrice said. She squinted in an attempt to catch a glimpse of her father's butler, but her childhood friend had already disappeared down the road.

"He always was crazy about you," Sally said. "But other than that, he's an absolute monster."

Beatrice pulled out a black-lace handkerchief and began wiping at the green mud stains that Horror had left on her dress when he hugged her. "Now I can show my face around the Manor again," Beatrice said. "I'm not a laughingstock."

Sally wanted to give her daughter a huge hug, but suddenly felt herself being pulled away, like a cloud on the wind.

A moment later, she found herself in the dingy, old Ghost Office, surrounded by some very angry-looking ghosts. They were chanting: "Hey-hey! Ho-ho! To the Next World we will go! Hey-hey! Ho-ho! Paperwork is much too slow!"

"What's going on?" Sally asked the ghost next to her.

"It's a protest!" the ghost explained. "We're sick of being ghosts—we want to go to the Next World now! Didn't you get the flyer?"

"No—I don't even know how I got here!"

"Oh—well, we managed to shove open the door to the Next World for a moment.

There was this huge rush of air—it blew the pink forms all over the room, like a cotton candy cyclone. It must have just sucked you in here."

Frank Farter and Harry Helmet were pushing against the door to the Next World, as Uriah Phantom tried to keep them away.

"Let us in!" Frank shouted. He pounded on the door, and it moved slightly. Papers and ghosts whirled around the room like confetti in a snow globe. Sally suddenly found herself standing directly in front of Uriah. One of the ghosts chucked his head into the Next World. (Unfortunately, the door closed a moment later, and the ghost's body ran around the office wildly until it banged into a wall and sat down.)

Uriah slammed the door closed—he was remarkably strong for such a transparent ghost—and shouted, "Fine! I'll let you in! But we have to proceed in an orderly fashion."

"You!" Uriah cried, pointing to Sally. "Hand over your documents."

Reluctantly, Sally handed over her papers, and Uriah scanned them. "Wonderful!" he cried. "Sally Mon Staire, I see that you have just made up with your daughter. This is perfect!" He applied an ACCEPTED stamp to the top part of the form.

BiNGo!!!

"Right this way," Uriah said, gesturing

toward the door to the Next World.

Sally bit her lip. She really didn't want to go to the Next World, even if it did look like Bermuda. She had just made up with her daughter. She wanted to enjoy it for a while.

"Well . . ." Sally hedged, "this is so sudden. I haven't packed a thing! Maybe we could wait a little while—it'll just take a year or so. . . ."

Uriah and the other ghosts glared at her. "You have one day," Uriah said crisply. "Or else I'll give you a curse that's even worse than Frank Furter's!"

"Farter!" Frank shouted.

"I know you are, but what am I?" Harry Helmet said. The rest of the ghosts cracked up.

"Next!" Uriah screeched as he pushed Sally out of the way.

And that was the end of that.

CHAPTER NINE
Sally's Plan

Sally looked up at the Manor door and sighed. She could hardly bear the thought that she had only one more day to spend with her friends. What was the point of going to the Next World, if it was only going to make her miserable? No, Sally decided, I have no choice. I have to make Beatrice mad at me again, so I can stay.

Sally floated up through the floor of Beatrice's room without knocking. Usually, that would have made her daughter furious. But not today.

"Mom!" Beatrice cried, grinning. She was sitting on her bed, surrounded by the rest of the monsters. "Thank goodness you're back! Do you have any ideas? We can't seem to wake these two up."

"These two" were Frankie and Professor Von Skalpel, both of whom were still snoring away.

Sally had an idea. She hated to do it, but she knew the perfect way to embarrass her daughter. "Sweetie, why don't you try one of your spells to wake them up?" Sally asked innocently, pointing to the dusty books on Beatrice's shelf.

Sally expected Beatrice to get furious at the suggestion. Beatrice knew that her mother didn't think much of her magical powers, and that she would only humiliate herself by trying to cast a spell in front of everyone.

"Mom, you're a genius!" Beatrice cried as she scanned the spines of the books, looking for one that might help. "Let's see. *The Encyclopedia Magicana*—too general. *Three-Hundred and Sixty-Five Recipes for Eye of Newt*—hmmm . . . I think we're out of newt. *Decorating with Black Magic*? There are a lot of good ideas in that one—but not for this. Ah—*Five Hundred Sorcerer-ish Thingamajigs and Whoseewhatsers for Everyday Problems*." Beatrice pulled the book from the shelf and flipped it open.

An enormous cloud of dust plumed from the book.

"I don't think this has been opened in twenty years," Beatrice said as she settled herself between Frankie and the professor and

blew more dust off the book. She flipped through the pages, and more dust rose, settling over everything and going straight up the monsters' noses. It was getting so hard to breathe that Beatrice pulled out her handkerchief and put it over her face.

Cough! Hack! Achoo!

"Blech!" the professor cried, sitting up. "Vhy do I feel like I am in a coal mine?"

Frankie sneezed again. And again. And again.

Beatrice grinned at her mother. "Way to go, Mom!" she shouted. "We woke them up!"

Sally gave her daughter a tight little smile.

It used to be so easy to make Beatrice mad at me! Now she's always happy with me, Sally thought. This is getting downright silly.

"Let's all go downstairs and have some breakfast!" Beatrice cried. A moment later, there was a sound like an earthquake on the stairs as the monsters followed her down to the kitchen.

Only two people were left in Beatrice's room. Sally stepped in front of the door to keep the professor from leaving.

The professor sneezed, then let out a small hiccup. "Vell, now zat I am avake, I have some very important vork to do. So, if you vill excuse me—"

"Not so fast," Sally said. "What were you planning with the robot?"

The professor turned bright red. "It's nothing—it is just . . . He vanted somezing zat belonged to your husband. I told him zat I vould hand it over at dawn."

Sally's eyes narrowed. "What did he want?"

"He did not tell me vhat it vas," Von Skalpel said, shaking his head. "Only vhere it vas. I guess it is some powerful, magical object."

"No wonder you were in such a hurry to get it," Sally said. "You wanted to try it out."

"No—I—"

Sally scowled at the professor, and he hung his head.

"Yes, it is true," he admitted.

"So where is this thing?" Sally asked.

Von Skalpel went into a coughing fit, then gestured toward the dresser. "Second drawer from zee top, in back, on zee right—it is in a little brown sack."

Sally yanked out the drawer and pulled out a brown paper bag. Reaching inside the bag, she pulled out a purple ball.

"Well, look at that!" Sally said with a

laugh. "Your magical object is a pair of purple socks." She laughed again and shook her head. "Actually, I'm amazed that he lived without his lucky socks for so long. He'll definitely send Harry the Robot back for these!" She glared at the professor. "And if he comes back before midnight, I'll give them to him myself," Sally said.

After all, it would be her last chance to say good-bye.

CHAPTER TEN
Sock It to Him!

"This is the best shoofly pie I've ever tasted," Horror said, as he dug into a thick, gooey slice.

The other monsters murmured in agreement. It was late in the evening, and everyone was gathered around the table for dessert. But they were all too busy munching pie to say much.

"The secret is the fresh flies," Sally said with a smile. She had trouble keeping the smile on her face, though. Even though the other monsters were in a wonderful mood (the television had been fixed that afternoon, and they all looked forward to watching that night's *Creature Feature*), Sally couldn't help feeling sad. She was the only one who knew that this was her last night in the Manor.

"Mom, this is delicious!" Beatrice said warmly, scraping the last crumb from her plate.

"It's excellent," Count Snobula agreed. Then he added, "I only wish that there were more." He gazed forlornly at the empty pie plate.

"There's another pie in the kitchen," Sally said quickly. "I'll get it."

Sally was busy cutting the pie into even slices when she heard the kitchen door swing open behind her. "Mrs. Mon Staire?" Frankie asked gently.

"Yes?"

"Is everything okay?" Frankie asked. "You seem sad tonight. Didn't your friend like my gift?"

"Oh, she loved it!" Sally said quickly. "It's just—" Sally's gaze flicked over Frankie's shoulder and landed on the wall clock: it was 11:30 P.M. already. "Listen," Sally said, changing the subject, "I've been thinking about your song—trying to find a rhyme for *rocks*. What about *socks*?"

Frankie tried it out:

Ooooh, you're so wonderful,
And I'm so blunderful,
Everything about you simply rocks!
Ooooh, you're so fabulous,
And I'm so scab-u-lous,
That we should . . . both exchange
    our socks.

"Wow," Frankie said, gazing at Sally. "That's really romantic. Exchanging socks—I have an old pair that are yellow, crusty, and full of holes—and I know that if someone gave me a new pair and took those away, well—that would be love."

"Yeah," Sally agreed, "and besides, it rhymes!"

Frankie rushed to give Sally a hug, but,

just then, the doorbell rang. Sally peered out the window and caught her breath. She had been expecting to see Harry the Robot, but the short stocky figure at the gate was none other than Allsaint Mon Staire!

Sally couldn't move. She couldn't bear to face her husband—how could she tell him that she was about to go to the Next World?

Sally looked down at the paper bag on the countertop and had a sudden idea. "Frankie," she said. "Would you do me a favor?" She motioned toward the window. "Do you see that man?"

Frankie nodded.

"Would you go outside and give him this pair of old socks?" Sally asked, holding out the paper bag. "And . . . would you tell him that they're from me, and that I still think about him?"

"Well, okay," Frankie said with a shrug. "As long as you promise to save me a piece of pie."

"I promise," Beatrice said.

Frankie walked out of the room, shaking his head and wondering about the man outside. The man was very well dressed, in a cape and a tall, silk hat. Frankie opened the bag and peered inside. The purple socks lay at the bottom, rolled into a ball. "Those are pretty nice socks," Frankie mumbled to himself. "It doesn't seem fair that Sally is just giving them away—especially since that guy outside is already pretty well dressed. He could buy his own socks!"

Sally stayed in the kitchen, staring out the window at Allsaint. He had hardly changed in the years that he had been gone. He still had googly eyes and only three strands of hair on his head. "As handsome as ever," Sally said with a sigh. She drummed her fingertips on the counter, wondering what was taking Frankie so long.

Frankie loped across the lawn and handed the sack to Allsaint, then seemed to stammer a few words. Allsaint didn't even glance toward the Manor. He just took his sock sack and walked down the road.

But when he reached the end of the road, Allsaint Mon Staire glared angrily at the Manor. "That's just like her!" he shouted.

"Sally and her silly practical jokes. I can't believe she'd give me these yellow, crusty, hole-filled things instead of my lucky purple socks!" Allsaint growled and tossed the gross socks into the ditch, then disappeared into the dark night, leaving the brilliant, noisy Manor behind.

Sally bit her lip and glanced at the clock: eleven forty-five. It was time to say good-bye to all her friends . . . and to her daughter. Sadly, Sally picked up the pie and headed toward the dining room.

Suddenly, a thick, purple cloud appeared in the room, and Uriah Phantom stepped through the refrigerator door.

"Wait— I haven't said good-bye yet!" Sally insisted. "You can't take me to the Next World. I still have fifteen minutes!"

Uriah simply scowled at Sally and handed her a large envelope.

"What's this?" Sally asked, ripping open the envelope. She scanned the page.

Re: Request for Passage,

Ghost Number 785.4848.6722

Dear Sally Mon Staire:

We regret to inform you that your request for passage to the Next World has been refused despite your recent reconciliation with your daughter. We remind you that you must be on good terms with everyone in your family. Since this is not the case, your request cannot be granted.

Sincerely,

I. M. Haunting

If Sally hadn't been a ghost, she might have dropped dead from surprise. "Does this mean that I don't have to go to the Next World?" she asked. "I can stay right here?"

Uriah shook his head. "I'm very sorry, but that's the way it has to be. Rules are rules." Then he stepped back through the refrigerator and disappeared.

Sally felt like singing. She didn't have to leave, after all! This was wonderful. She picked up the pie and hurried into the dining room, chirping, "Who wants another slice?"

"I do!" all of the monsters chorused.

"Thanks, Mom," Beatrice said as she took a slice. "This looks fantastic."

Sally's eyebrows drew together in confusion. I don't get it, Sally thought. Beatrice still isn't mad at me. So—who is? Great Aunt

Nancy? Nah—she was always crazy about me. It just doesn't make sense.

"This pie tastes better than the mailman!" Wolf Man Stu shouted as he dug in.

Sally helped herself to a slice of pie and decided not to worry about who could be mad at her. Clearly, it wasn't anyone there at the Manor. Besides, she got to stay where she wanted, and that was all that mattered.

And from that day forward, Sally became Frankie's songwriting assistant. She helped him come up with a few rhymes for his number one hit, "I Just Love My New Purple Socks!"

Of course, Sally never figured out that the song was actually about the socks Frankie was supposed to have given to Allsaint earlier.

Then again, she never really thought about it very much. She was too busy having fun with her friends at the Manor . . . where she belonged.